Roses Are Red

Kenzie Skye

ONE

Selene

Rain speckles my skin as I saunter down the slick streets, the drizzle a mere whisper against the immortality of my flesh. The neon chaos of the metropolis pulses around me—a symphony of cerulean, magenta, and electric lime that dances in reflections on the pavement. My eyes, crystalline blue and sharp as the edge of night, catch every flickering shadow, every potential prey that skulks in this urban jungle.

Hunger coils within me, tight and insistent, but it's not just for the warm, sweet rush of blood tonight. No, there's a deeper craving gnawing at the core of me—a yearning that's rooted in the marrow of my ancient bones.

For centuries, I've walked these paths, cloaked in beauty and power, a predator among sheep. Yet beneath this alabaster skin and the cascade of moonlit hair lies a heart weary from the relentless march of time. Solitude has been my only constant companion, its cold embrace more intimate than any lover's touch.

Another night. Another fleeting taste of life that isn't mine to keep.

I glide past throngs of mortals, their lives burning so fiercely bright and oh-so-ephemeral. They're ignorant of the darkness that shimmers at the periphery of their vision—the darkness that I am. Every beat of their hearts is a drumroll to my senses, every pulse a siren call.

Is this all there is? The thought creeps in unbidden, a shadow stretching over the glow of my existence. It's a dangerous question—one that could unravel the fabric of what I've become. But it haunts me nonetheless, a ghostly refrain that keeps pace with the staccato rhythm of my heels against the wet street.

With each step, I feel the weight of countless

decades resting upon my shoulders, a mantle woven from isolation and the silken threads of unspoken desires. What I wouldn't give for a single moment of genuine connection, a spark to ignite the tinder of my soul and set it ablaze with something more...something real.

Enough. I chide myself, shaking off the melancholy like droplets from the rain. Tonight isn't about existential brooding. It's about survival, about the hunt.

And yet, as I prowl through the city's veins, I can't help but wonder if amidst this sea of humanity, there might be someone who could understand the eternity etched in my gaze.

The neon glow splinters across the pavement, a fractured rainbow slick with rain, as I slip through the crowd. People are blurs of color and noise, their heartbeats thrumming in my ears like a relentless drum, promising life, promising warmth.

But then, a mortal catches my eye.

He's all effortless motion, this man, threading his way through the masses with an ease that speaks of innate self-assurance. He's unaware of the shadows that cling to the edges of this world.

Of creatures like me who watch from the darkness.

His routine seems so mundane, so deliciously human. A touch to his watch, a glance at the street signs, every step taken with purpose. Yet he's anything but ordinary. There's a confidence to him that sets my senses alight, a vibrancy that beckons me closer.

I can't help it. I'm drawn in, like a moth to flame. With each step he takes, I feel a pull, an invisible thread winding around my cold, undead heart. It's ludicrous, this sensation, this raw curiosity that blooms within me. It's dangerous—for him, for me.

He continues on, blissfully ignorant of my gaze.

He stops at a crosswalk, the light painting him in shades of urgency—red, yellow, green. Go, it signals, and he does, with a fluidity that's more dance than walk. My eyes never stray, and there's a tightness in my chest that's been absent for centuries.

Two

Marcus

The night air nips at my skin, but I don't feel the cold—not really. It's more like a whisper of sensation, a footnote to the buzz of life around me. I'm just a regular guy in a city that never sleeps, caught up in the usual ebb and flow of midnight ramblers and neon dreamers. That is, until *she* steps into view.

She's a walking contradiction—ethereal yet grounded in shadows that seem to cling to her like adoring fans. My eyes trace the curve of her cheek, the smooth line of her neck, and for a moment, everything else fades out. There's this pull, like a hook lodged deep in my gut, drawing me towards her.

Who are you? The question slips through my mind, unvoiced but loud as hell. She looks like someone who could make angels sin or devils pray. And damn, if she isn't the most beautiful thing I've ever seen under the hazy city lights.

I follow her because, well, what else am I going to do? She moves with a purpose I can't fathom, a beauty in high heels. I tell myself it's just curiosity. That's all.

Then it happens. She corners someone—a guy, alone, probably drunk—in an alley. I hang back, a voyeur to the scene unfolding. There's a dance to it—an intimacy that sends a flare of jealousy through me. Jealousy? Since when do I get jealous over strangers?

But then her mouth is on his neck, and it's not a lover's kiss. It's savage, brutal. The sound of ripping flesh tears through the quiet, followed by a choked-off scream that ends as suddenly as it began. Blood—glistening, dark, so much blood—spills onto the concrete, mingling with rainwater in a macabre painting.

"Jesus..." The word escapes me, a breathless exhalation. This isn't some late-night hook-up. This is primal, raw, a nature documentary with the veneer stripped away. My heart thuds against my ribcage, a trapped bird desperate for escape.

And still, I can't tear my eyes away from her. Her beauty's unchanged, undimmed by the violence. How can something so horrific be wrapped up in such a stunning package? The dichotomy screws with my head, sets every nerve ending on fire.

"Fuck," I mutter, backing away, my feet clumsy, my brain screaming at me to run. Yet part of me doesn't want to leave, wants to understand, to dive into the darkness that swirls around her like a cloak.

What kind of man does that make me? What kind of creature is she?

I stumble backward, my shoe catching on a jagged edge of sidewalk. It's like my body's caught in a glitch, movements jerky and out of sync with the chaos churning inside my head. She stands there, blood painting her lips in a crimson smear that glistens under the flickering streetlamp. It's straight out of a horror flick—only there's no screen to separate me from the nightmare.

"Fuck me sideways," I hiss, pressing a hand against the cold wall for support. The world tilts dangerously, reality skewing into realms of impossibility. I've stumbled into some twisted urban fantasy, except this is no fantasy. It's too visceral, too goddamn real.

She licks her lips, and it's obscene, the way that simple gesture makes my gut twist. Not in revulsion, but with an inexplicable pull of attraction that's got no right being here, not now. Bloodlust and lust-lust are getting their wires crossed in my brain.

I turn then, finally letting instinct take over, and I run. I run through the rain-slicked streets, neon lights blurring into streaks of color, heart pounding a frantic beat. And behind me, I can almost feel her smile, wide and full of secrets, chasing me into the night.

THREE

Marcus

The night pulses with secrets, and I can't shake the itch to peel back its layers. What I've seen...it's not something you just forget. Ghostly whispers in the dark, shadows that move against the grain of reality—they gnaw at my mind, demanding answers.

Her. She's a riddle wrapped in a mystery inside an enigma, and damn if she isn't the most captivating part of the puzzle. As she glides through the rain-slicked streets, the city lights catch in her icy blue eyes, casting luminescent paths that beckon me closer. Her hair, a cascade of moonlight, seems to float around her, untouched by the dampness that clings to everything else in this metropolis.

I lean against the cool brick of a nearby building, trying to seem casual, but I'm anything but. The way she moves...it's like she's part of the night itself. There's a grace to her steps that's more than human, a silent melody that only the darkest corners of the world could hum. And for some godforsaken reason, I want to hum along.

She's the kind of fire that doesn't just burn—it *consumes*. There's an air of danger about her, a promise of peril that makes every nerve ending stand at attention. She's the embodiment of every warning I've ever ignored, every line I've crossed in pursuit of the thrill. She's temptation incarnate, and I can't help but step off the curb to follow.

Selene pauses at the mouth of an alley, her profile etched against the neon glow of the city. Even from here, I can feel the magnetic pull, the electric charge in the air that crackles between us. She turns, as if sensing my gaze, and I swear the world tilts on its axis.

"Gotcha," I whisper, though I'm not sure if I'm the hunter or the hunted.

She's otherworldly, and it hits me right in the gut

—the raw, unexplainable draw to peel back her layers and discover what lies beneath. It's not just her beauty. It's the enigma, the power that vibrates in the space she occupies. She's a puzzle I'm itching to solve, even if it means getting lost in the dark.

I'm tailing her, close but not too close. The city hums around us, a discordant symphony of car horns and distant chatter, but it's like we're in our own bubble of silence. She moves with the grace of a shadow, slipping through the crowds that part for her without knowing why.

"Damn," I mutter under my breath. She's the perfect blend of danger and desire, wrapped up in an enigma that's got my heart pumping double time. Every instinct screams at me to chase the mystery, to dive headfirst into whatever rabbit hole she's leading me down.

And then, as if fate throws me a bone, she drops a glove—slender, black leather, like something out of a noir film. I snatch it up, the leather not warm from her touch as it should be, and hustle to catch up.

"Hey!" I call out, waving the glove. "You dropped this!"

She turns, those icy blue eyes locking onto mine, and it's like a kick to the chest. My pulse races, every sense on high alert. There's something electric in the moment, a current that surges through me, connecting us.

"Thanks," she says, her voice a melody that sends shivers down my spine. Her fingers brush mine as she takes the glove, and it's all I can do not to grab her and pull her close. But there's caution in her gaze, a guarded edge that tells me she's not one to be trifled with.

"Careless of me," she adds, a ghost of a smile on her lips that doesn't quite reach her eyes.

"Happy to help," I shoot back, trying to sound smoother than I feel. "Name's Marcus. And you are...?"

"Selene." Just one word, but it's loaded with a thousand secrets.

We stand there for a heartbeat too long, the air charged with something unspoken. It's crazy, but I swear I can almost hear her thoughts, feel the weight of what she's holding back.

"Nice to meet you, Selene."

"Likewise, Marcus."

And then she's off again, melting into the crowd. But this time, I don't follow. Something tells me I'll be seeing her again soon.

Very soon.

Four

Selene

From behind my veil of normalcy, I watch Marcus retreat, his confident stride belying the intrigue I've sparked within him. He's different, this human, with his piercing green eyes and aura of resilience. The way he looks at me, as though he sees beyond the facade, is unnerving.

The risk is monumental. Revealing what I am could send him screaming into the night—or worse, it could put us both in grave danger.

For centuries, I've walked alone, an apex predator cloaked in moonlight and myth. The thought of sharing my darkness with someone... it's intoxicating and terrifying in equal measure.

Is he worth the gamble? I feel the ancient curse of my kind heavy on my shoulders. The loneliness is a familiar ache, one I've numbed over time, but Marcus stirs something within me that's been dormant for far too long.

"Damn it," I curse softly. The pull towards him is undeniable. It defies logic, flies in the face of centuries of self-preservation.

But for the first time in an eternity, I'm tempted to lay my cards on the table and show him the monster beneath the beauty.

Somehow, I know our paths will cross again—and when they do, I'll have to make a choice that could change everything.

———

The rain has stopped, but the city's pulse quickens under the cloak of night. I find myself on a deserted street that seems to throb with invisible energy. It's here that I sense him again—Marcus, the mortal that has haunted my thoughts.

"Selene?" His voice comes from the shadows, a rich baritone that sends a shiver down my spine.

I turn, and there he stands, soaked in silver light. Without a word, I close the distance between us, drawn by a force beyond my control.

"Marcus," I whisper, my breath a misty cloud in the cool air.

"I've been following you for days," he admits.

"I know," I acknowledge simply.

We stare at one another. I study Marcus. Handsome. Curious. I should sense fear, but I don't.

I consider.

Fuck it.

"There's something you need to know about me."

He watches me intently, his piercing green eyes reflecting a curiosity that matches my own. I reach for his hand, guiding it to my lips. I kiss his knuckles, my cold touch belying the fire that rages within me —a fire that burns for revelation, for liberation.

"Tell me," he urges, his voice barely above a murmur, laced with desire and anticipation.

"Close your eyes," I instruct, and he complies. The trust he exhibits stirs a warmth in me that I had long forgotten, a flicker of humanity amidst the eternal chill.

"Listen to the night," I say, my voice a sultry

melody. "Can you hear it? The symphony of the unseen, the whispers of the ageless."

He nods, his Adam's apple bobbing slightly. "I can feel it... around you. It's like you're part of it."

"Because I am," I confess, my fingers trailing up his arm, raising goosebumps on his flesh. "I am the night, Marcus. I am what lurks in the heart of darkness. What walks in dreams and preys upon the living."

"Show me," he breathes out, his words a caress against my skin.

With a fluid grace, I step back, releasing him from my touch. My heart races—though it doesn't beat—as I prepare to drop the veil. A look of concentration passes over my face as I muster the courage, and then, I let go.

"Open your eyes, Marcus," I command softly.

When he does, I stand transformed before him. My eyes, now glowing icy blue, lock onto his. Fangs extend, sharp and glistening, a testament to my true nature. My moonlit hair cascades around me, an ethereal frame to the monster I've revealed.

"Selene..." His voice is a mixture of awe and disbelief. "You're...you're...a..."

"Vampire," I finish for him, the word a velvet caress in the silence.

He takes a tentative step forward, his fascination clear in the way his eyes drink in my changed form. "Incredible," he murmurs, reaching out to trace the line of my jaw.

"Are you afraid?" I ask, my voice low and tinged with the centuries of loneliness that have shadowed my existence.

"Of death? Perhaps," he replies, his hand steady. "But of you? Never."

His acceptance is a flame that ignites something primal within me. I move closer, until our bodies are nearly touching, the heat of his alive against the cold of my undead.

"Then welcome to my world, Marcus Leclair."

FIVE

Selene

I glide through the labyrinthine hallways of my lair, Marcus in tow, his heartbeat a syncopated rhythm that thrums in time with my own. The air is thick, charged with a current that could power a city, if not for the fact that it's just us, here, alone in the dark.

"Where are we going?" he asks, a hint of excitement lacing his words, his green eyes glinting like emeralds in the moonlight slipping through the cracks.

"To someplace special," I tease, my voice a velvety

purr that hangs in the shadows. I can feel the heat radiating off him, the living pulse of his blood calling to me like a siren song. It's a melody I've heard countless times over my long years, but with Marcus, it sings a new verse, one filled with a raw desire that's hard to ignore.

We reach the end of the corridor, and I push open an ornate door that creaks softly on its hinges. We step into a chamber where the light dances across the walls, candles flickering as if they're whispering secrets to each other. The room smells of jasmine and old books, a scent that's as intoxicating as the finest blood.

"Wow," Marcus breathes out, and I can't help but smile at the awe in his voice.

"Like it?" I ask, my gaze sweeping the room, taking in the plush rugs that cushion our steps, the rich tapestries that tell tales of another age, and the velvet drapes that hold back the night.

"It's incredible," he murmurs, turning to me, his gaze hungry. "*You're* incredible."

The compliment warms something inside me, something I thought had gone cold centuries ago. I watch him drink in the sight before us, his curiosity a live wire sparking between us.

"Make yourself comfortable," I say, though it's

more of an invitation, a challenge. How far will he go? How close will he dare to come?

"Comfortable?" His laugh is a low chuckle that seems to reverberate against my skin. "I don't know if that's possible right now, considering the company."

"Flatterer," I accuse, though I'm secretly pleased. For a moment, we simply stand there, two beings caught in a moment so fragile, it feels like the world outside this chamber has ceased to exist.

I gesture toward the couch, the velvet as dark as a raven's wing, and it's like I'm offering him more than just a place to sit. It's an invitation into my world, my heart, maybe even my bed. That thought alone sends a wicked thrill spiraling through me.

"Sit," I command with a smirk, keeping it light, keeping it easy. But who am I kidding? The air is thick with everything unsaid, everything we're on the brink of discovering about each other.

He sinks into the cushions, his body a study in casual elegance, and I perch beside him. Close, but not too close. God, his warmth is a tangible thing, and I wonder if he feels the chill emanating from my own flesh.

"Tell me something true," I dare him, my voice soft as shadows.

"True?" He quirks an eyebrow, that green gaze of

his sharp and searching. "I've always wanted to know what forever looks like."

"Forever is overrated," I quip back, quick as a heartbeat. "

We trade tales like cards, each story a piece of ourselves laid bare. I tell him of centuries spent walking through empires turned to dust, of loves lost like whispers in the wind. He gives me his dreams of the future, bright and bold and so damn beautiful it hurts to hear them.

The candlelight dances across the room, flickering in a rhythm that mirrors the erratic beat of my undead heart. Marcus sits there, his green eyes alight with stories and laughter, and I find myself drawn to the heat of his presence.

"Ever dance with the devil by the pale moonlight?" I tease, the words slipping out more as an invitation than a jest.

"Only if the devil looks like you," he shoots back, a playful smirk tugging at the corners of his lips.

Our banter is a thin veil over the tension that crackles between us like static. With each confession, each shared laugh, the ice around my heart melts a little more. The chill of centuries begins to feel like a mere prelude to the warmth I see reflected in his gaze.

"Marcus," I whisper, my voice barely above the

sound of our breathing, "you don't know what you're getting into."

"Then enlighten me," he urges, leaning in so close that I can feel the whisper of his breath against my skin. It's warm, alive, everything I'm not...and everything I crave.

In a moment of reckless abandon or maybe just human—no, vampiric—longing, I let slip a truth I've kept hidden for too long. "I fear," I confess, my voice quivering like a leaf in the breeze, "that one day, this eternity will swallow me whole, and I'll be nothing but a shadow lost in the dark."

"Never," he says fiercely, his conviction ringing clear and true. "You burn too brightly to ever fade away."

He reaches out, hand trembling just slightly, as if he's afraid I might shatter under his touch. His fingers brush against my cheek, cool against his warmth, and my breath catches. It's a strange sensation, being touched by someone whose life force pulsates so vividly. A shiver runs down my spine, not from cold, but from the sheer intensity of feeling him so near.

"Your skin," he murmurs, tracing the line of my jaw, "it's like marble...yet there's a fire beneath it. A fire I want to stoke until it roars."

His words are a spark to my kindling, and I realize that this moment is dangerous—not because of what I am, but because of what I *want*. I want to lean into his touch, to feel his pulse pounding alongside mine, to revel in the rush of desire that courses through me, unnatural for my kind but oh so deliciously human.

"Marcus," I breathe out, caught in the gravity of his gaze, "you're playing with fire."

"Then let me burn," he replies, the raw edge in his voice betraying the depth of his yearning.

The room suddenly feels smaller, the walls closing in on us, encasing us in a world where only we exist. There's no past haunting me, no future taunting him. There's just *now*, this electric now, and the impossible man who's reaching straight into the heart of me.

I place my hands against Marcus's chest, feeling the solid beat of his heart under my palms. "Wait," I say, and there's a tremble in my voice that I don't like. The strength it takes to push him back is more than physical—it's the force of will against the pull of desire.

"Selene?" He's questioning, puzzled, as he studies my face. "What's wrong?"

"Marcus," I start, my words laced with an

urgency that makes them heavier than I intend. "This, us...it's not just complicated. It's dangerous." I step back, putting space between the heat of his body and the chill of mine. The air crackles with the tension of unsaid words and unspent passion.

"Every story has its villains, but mine..." My laugh is brittle, like ice on the verge of shattering. "Well, they're literally out for blood. My enemies are relentless and cruel. And if you get tangled up in my world, you won't just get burned, you'll be scorched."

He frowns, the lines around his eyes deepening, those striking green eyes that remind me of the verdant forests I haven't walked in centuries. "Let me worry about that," he says, stepping closer again, undaunted.

"Damn it, Marcus!" I snap, frustration and fear bleeding into my tone. "You don't understand! They would tear you apart without a second thought. You're mortal—vibrant and alive—and that makes you vulnerable. To them, you're nothing more than collateral damage."

"Then teach me," he fires back, his resilience shining through, "how to survive in your world. I can learn. I can fight."

"Learning to fight isn't the point." I'm pacing now, my movements sharp and erratic. "Even if you could stand against them, why should you have to? For what? A fleeting moment with a creature like me? It's not worth your life, Marcus."

"Who says it's fleeting?" His voice is soft but insistent, reaching for something beyond the physical draw between us.

"History," I say flatly, stopping to lock eyes with him. "My history. I've lived lifetimes, Marcus. What seems like forever to you is merely a heartbeat to me. I cannot ask you to risk everything for a heartbeat."

"Maybe I'm willing to risk it," he counters, and there's a fervor in his eyes that almost sways me.

Almost.

"Marcus," I whisper, my own longing spilling over, making my next words ache as I speak them. "You don't know what you're asking for."

But he's already too close, and I'm afraid of how much I want to let him stay.

I bite my lip, the taste of iron on my tongue as I watch the resolve harden in Marcus's gaze. He steps closer again, undaunted by the darkness that clings to my very essence.

"Selene," he says, his voice a low rumble that

vibrates through the velvet air between us. "I've seen the night in your eyes, felt the chill of your touch, and still, I stand here, craving more than just whispers in the shadows."

His words slice through my defenses, raw and real, more penetrating than any blade. I want to scoff, to remind him of the gulf between our existences, but instead, I find myself drowning in the sincerity of his plea.

"Marcus, you don't understand," I start, but he cuts me off with a passion that sends a shiver down my spine.

"I understand enough," he insists, stepping into my personal space, close enough that I can feel the heat emanating from his body. "I understand that being with you might be lethal, but not being with you...that's a slow death I refuse to endure."

My heart, a dormant creature for far too long, stirs at his confession. His determination—foolish though it may be—touches something deep within me, something I thought was lost to the ages.

"Your love...it's a reckless thing," I murmur, my voice barely louder than the flickering candlelight around us.

"Maybe," he concedes with a half-smile that

doesn't quite reach his eyes. "But it's mine to give, and I give it freely, Selene. To you, and only you."

The longing in his expression mirrors the ache in my chest, an echo of emotions I've long since buried. I let my façade slip, just for a moment, letting him glimpse the turbulence beneath my icy exterior.

"Marcus..." The word is a sigh, a lamentation, heavy with all the reasons we should keep our distance. But there's a part of me—a reckless, foolish part—that yearns to believe in the impossible.

"Look at me," he urges, lifting my chin with fingers that tremble ever so slightly. His green eyes are oceans of resolve, and I'm sinking, sinking fast. "Tell me you don't feel this too."

I do. Eternity help me, I do. If Marcus was a vampire, I'd swear he was my mate. I barely know him, yet it feels like I've known him forever. I am drawn to him in ways I can't understand.

And that's why I can't allow any harm to come to him. I thought I could do this. Thought I could steal just one fleeting moment of pleasure and send him on his way, but I can't.

"Feeling isn't the issue," I say, my tone softening despite my best efforts. "It's the consequences that terrify me. Not for myself, but for you."

"Let me worry about the consequences," he whispers, so close now that his breath caresses my lips. "I'm not afraid, Selene."

And as I stand there, caught in the unwavering depth of his gaze, I wonder if maybe—just maybe—I could allow myself the luxury of forgetting fear, if only for the briefest of moments.

Six

Selene

But then I come back to my senses. A shiver runs up my spine, not from the chill in the air—what's cold to a vampiress?—but from Marcus's piercing gaze, so full of heat it could melt the frost off my heart. He's too close, too much, and it scares the hell out of me.

"Marcus, you don't get it," I say, pulling away just enough to breathe. My voice is a whisper of silk against skin, an attempt at levity when what I really feel is panic. "I'm like... like a drug. An enchantment. You can't trust what you're feeling because—"

"Stop." His interruption is vehement, his hands cupping my face with such tenderness it stings. "Don't put this on some supernatural spell. It's not your allure that drew me in."

My laugh is a brittle sound, sharp enough to cut. "Oh, come on. I'm a creature of the night. I'm designed to lure unsuspecting mortals to their doom—or at least to their moral corruption."

He's having none of it. "Bullshit." The word is blunt, a verbal slap that jolts me. Marcus leans in, all fierce determination and raw honesty. "There's something about you, Selene. Something more than beauty or power. It's *you*—the woman who laughs at my bad jokes and dances in the shadows like she owns them."

"Marcus..." I try to warn him off again, but the words die on my lips. Because damn it, he's making sense. And it feels too good to hear someone say those things about me.

"Listen to me," he urges, green eyes blazing. "I've never felt this way about anyone before. Not like this. It's wild and terrifying and utterly real. I don't care if you're a goddess or a monster or anything in between. I want *you*, Selene. All of you. Every dark corner, every hidden scar."

His words should frighten me, send me

running to the safety of solitude. Instead, they wrap around me like a lover's embrace, warm and inviting. I'm lost in the sincerity of his confession, drowning in the possibility that maybe there's truth in his touch.

"Damn you, Marcus Leclair," I murmur, and whether it's a curse or a benediction, I don't know. What I do know is that resisting him is becoming the hardest battle I've ever fought. And for a vampire centuries old, that's saying something.

I stand uncertainly for the first time in centuries, the space between us charged with a raw energy that threatens to consume me. He's close, too close, his warmth radiating like a beacon in the chill of my chamber. I can feel the thrumming of his heartbeat, a rhythm that sings of life and tempts the predator within.

"Marcus," I shake my head as if to clear it of the fog my want has induced, my voice low and fractured by the storm of emotions brewing inside me. "You have to go."

He blinks, confusion etched across those striking features. "Go? Selene, after everything we've just—"

"Exactly because of everything." My words cut through the dense air, sharp and final. I step back, putting distance between temptation and duty.

"Being with me...it's not just dangerous. It's a death wish."

"Then let them come." His jaw sets, that damned determination making him all the more irresistible. "I'm not afraid."

"Of course you aren't," I snap, a bitter laugh escaping me. "You're human, Marcus. Brave and beautifully reckless. But you don't understand the forces that hunt me."

"Then explain it to me. We'll face them together."

I shake my head, moonlight hair cascading around my shoulders in a silvery wave. "It's not that simple. This isn't some fairy tale where love conquers all. They will destroy you, and I can't...I won't be the reason your light is snuffed out."

"Selene, please." The plea in his voice nearly breaks me, but I harden my resolve.

"Listen to me!" The command in my tone surprises even me. "You think this is about fear? It's not. It's about eternity. An eternity of watching people I dare to care for wither and die. And I can't do that again. Not with you."

"Then turn me." The suggestion hangs heavy between us, forbidden and tempting.

"Turn you?" I repeat, incredulous. "You don't want that, trust me. You think immortality is a gift?

It's a curse, one I wouldn't wish on my worst enemy, let alone..."

"Let alone what? Someone you care for?" He steps closer, bridging the gap I'd so carefully placed between us.

"Damn it, Marcus!" My hands ball into fists at my sides. "Why can't you see? I'm trying to save you from me. From the monster I am."

"Then slay your monsters with me. I'm not leaving you to fight alone."

"Because you don't get it!" Tears sting my eyes, and I hate how they betray the turmoil inside. "You're not safe here. Not with me, not anywhere near my world. And as long as you're alive, there's hope. Hope that you'll find someone who can give you the life you deserve, one without shadows and blood and endless night."

"Selene—" His protest is cut short as I step forward, placing a finger against his lips.

"Shh. Listen," I say, softer now but no less firm. "You need to leave. Now. Before they come. Before I change my mind."

"Is this really what you want?"

"It's what I need," I whisper, the words slicing through me. "It's what you need, too, even if you don't see it yet."

"Selene..."

"Go, Marcus." My voice trembles, but I bolster it with every ounce of strength I possess. "Please. For both our sakes."

He searches my gaze, looking for the lie he hopes to find. But all he sees is the truth of my conviction. Reluctantly, he nods, the weight of defeat bowing his shoulders. He turns, each step away another crack in the fragile façade I maintain.

"Remember me," he says without looking back.

"Always," I reply, though the word is barely a breath, lost in the shadows that reclaim him.

The door closes, and I'm alone once more, surrounded by the eerie silence of my lair. I sink onto the couch, its plush comfort cold against the sudden emptiness inside me. I've done the right thing, made the noble choice.

So why does it feel like I've just ripped out my own heart?

SEVEN

Marcus

I wake up with the dawn, Selene's image burned into my eyelids. Her icy gaze, her moonlit hair —it's like she's branded onto my senses. I roll out of bed, throw on some clothes. Can't waste time. Today's another shot at finding her.

I tried to honor her wishes, but I can't.

God help me, I can't.

She's all I think about. All I dream about.

I've fucking *obsessed*.

I've got to find her.

The city is a different beast in the early hours, all

soft edges and sleepy murmurs. I hit the pavement, tracking back to where it all began—the alley where we first met. It's deserted now, the thrill of last night replaced by the mundane push of morning routines.

"Hey man, you seen a woman around here?" I ask a street cleaner, trying to sound casual. "Blue eyes, hair's like...well, like the full moon decided to get sexy on her head." He just shrugs, pushing his cart past me.

"Sorry, buddy," he mumbles as he shoots me a curious look.

"Figures," I mutter under my breath, moving on.

Coffee shop next, the one with the barista who gives me knowing looks over steaming cups of joe. "Morning, Marcus," she greets me, already prepping my usual.

"Morning," I reply, leaning on the counter. "Hey, you ever see a woman come through here? Looks like she walked straight out of a fairytale? Blue eyes that could freeze hell over?"

The barista pauses, a frown creasing her brow. "Can't say I have. But I'll keep an eye out."

"Thanks," I say, drumming my fingers on the countertop. It's not like I expected it to be easy, but damn, this is like hunting smoke.

I take my coffee to go, wandering through the

streets, hitting every place I can think of. The park, the bridge under the starlight, the corner where she vanished into thin air. I canvass them all, asking anyone who might have seen a creature as mesmerizing as Selene.

"Excuse me," I approach an old man feeding pigeons, "ever spot a woman around here who looks like she could turn the world on its head with just a glance?"

He chuckles, tossing crumbs to the birds. "Son, if I had, I'd be following her myself."

"Right," I sigh. This is getting me nowhere fast.

But I can't give up, not when every fiber of my being screams her name. I'm out here chasing shadows because whatever Selene is, whatever danger she brings with her, I *need* that fire. I need her mystery, her allure. And I won't stop until I find her again.

I push deeper into the city's heart, where the sun hesitates to tread.

"Seen a woman with moonlit hair and blue eyes?" I ask a street artist. He shrugs before he dips his brush back into the night sky he's painting onto the wall.

"Art like that doesn't walk around here," he says,

and I can't help but agree. Selene is art, but she's alive, deadly, and I'm hooked.

The alleyways twist and turn, a labyrinth designed to disorient. But it's not just the layout that's got my head spinning. It's the lack of her. Not a whisper, not a shadow that matches hers.

Frustration gnaws at me, turning my insides into a tangled mess. This search is starting to feel like a wild chase after a wisp of smoke—elusive, maddening.

And then, like a sign, there they are—roses. A vendor at the corner has them lined up like little soldiers in shades of passion and blood. My feet move before I even decide, drawn to the vivid reds that scream Selene's name without saying a word.

"Give me the best one you've got," I tell the vendor, my voice low and rough with more emotions than I care to untangle right now.

He eyes me with a knowing look, a smirk dancing on his lips as he picks out a rose with petals as deep as a heartache. "For someone special?" he asks, wrapping the stem carefully to protect me from its thorns.

"Something like that," I say, my mind already racing ahead to how I'll leave it for her, a silent confession, a plea. A single red rose, because damn if that doesn't scream 'desire' louder than any words I could muster.

I pay him with a couple of crumpled bills and a nod, tucking the rose inside my jacket like it's a secret. Or maybe it's more like a talisman, something to keep me sane while I wander this concrete jungle looking for a vampiress who's probably more myth than woman.

But myths don't leave you burning, do they? They don't sear their image into your retinas or lace your dreams with whispers of eternity. No, Selene's real alright. And this rose, it's going to lead me right back to her. I can feel it.

The chill of the night air nips at my skin as I slide through the streets, the rose's stem pressing against my chest through the fabric of my jacket. It's a silent heartbeat, an echo of my own that drums a wild rhythm of anticipation. Selene's lair looms ahead, a place where shadows pool like ink and whispers of the ancient cling to the worn stones.

I pause at her door, the grandeur of it mocking my mortal hesitations. But screw it—I'm here now, aren't I? With a steadiness I don't feel, I reach inside my jacket and pull out the red rose. It's perfect, untouched by the night, petals dark and luscious against the pale moonlight.

"Here goes nothing," I mutter under my breath, leaning forward to place the rose on her doorstep. The stone is cold beneath my fingers, but I swear I can feel the thrumming energy of the lair, like a pulse waiting to be quickened by her presence. This rose—it's more than a symbol. It's a promise, a raw confession of desire etched in crimson.

I step back, retreating into the shroud of darkness, my back pressed against the rough texture of the alley wall. The city hums around me, but I am cocooned in this pocket of silence, a sentinel of longing in the quiet before the dawn.

My gaze fixates on the entrance to her domain, every sense straining for a sign. The thought of her finding the rose, of her knowing—really knowing—how deeply she's gotten under my skin, sends a thrill racing down my spine. I imagine those icy blue eyes softening just a fraction, that marble-carved face giving way to curiosity or even...could it be? Affection?

Time warps around me, minutes stretching into lifetimes as I linger, waiting for any hint of movement. I can almost smell her scent, that intoxicating blend of night-blooming flowers and something indefinably wild, woven through the crisp air.

"Come on, Selene," I whisper to the emptiness,

my voice threaded with impatience and a hunger that's got nothing to do with food.

But the night remains stubbornly still, and I'm left with the ghost of her touch burning in my veins, both torment and solace as I stand watch. My every nerve ending is alive with the possibility of her, with the maddening allure of the supernatural creature who's claimed me without even trying.

Patience has never been my strong suit, especially not when it comes to matters of the heart—or whatever tangled web this is.

And yet, here I am, playing the world's most twisted game of hide-and-seek with a vampiress who's probably centuries older than the concept of games themselves. If that isn't a testament to the power she holds over me, I don't know what is.

So I wait, hidden in the embrace of the shadows, a man bewitched, betting it all on a single red rose.

EIGHT

Marcus

I shove my hands deep into my pockets and stalk away from her lair, the grittiness of the city's heartbeat failing to match my own erratic pulse. Hours have dragged by, each second a taunt, each shadow a tease of Selene's absence. My patience is frayed at the edges, torn apart by the silence that answers my silent calls to her.

"Food," I mutter to myself, the word strange and hollow as it echoes off the empty streets. I need something mundane, something achingly normal to anchor me back to reality—even if just for a fleeting moment. A hole-in-the-wall diner blares neon promise, and I slide onto a barstool, the vinyl squeaking beneath me like a living thing.

"Hit me with your greasiest burger," I tell the waitress, a tired sort with a smile that doesn't quite reach her eyes. She nods, unfazed by the urgency in my voice. "And keep the coffee coming."

I tear into the food with more gusto than taste, barely registering the flavors. It's fuel, nothing more. My mind is elsewhere, tangled up with images of icy blue eyes and hair that seems spun from the very essence of night itself. Even here, surrounded by the clatter of dishes and the low murmur of late-night patrons, I feel her. It's like she's perched on the edge of my consciousness, watching me with that unnerving stillness of hers.

The meal is over too quickly, or maybe not quickly enough. The restlessness has me tapping my fingers against the laminate countertop, itching to get moving again. I toss a few crumpled bills down and push myself out into the cooling night air.

Back at Selene's lair, the anticipation winds tight in my chest, a spring coiling, ready to snap. I scan the area, my gaze hungry for any sign of her, any hint that the rose was more than just a splash of color against the relentless grey of the city. The doorstep is as I left it, but there's an energy in the air, a charge that sends shivers racing along my spine.

I can almost feel her laughter, a whisper of sound that is felt rather than heard.

I'm on the verge of throwing in the towel, my feet sore and spirit bordering on defeat. The dim light from the streetlamps casts long shadows, playing tricks on my eyes, making me see things that aren't there—or so I think.

Then, just as I start doubting myself, there's a flicker, a ripple in the darkness that snags my attention. My head whips around, and for one heart-stopping moment I see her—Selene, shrouded in mystery, standing there like some moonlit vision. Those icy blue eyes pierce through the gloom, sending a jolt of electricity down my spine.

"Selene?" My voice cracks the silence, hopeful, desperate.

But as quick as a blink, she's gone, vanished into the shadows from which she emerged.

Was she ever really there?

Damn it, she's got me second-guessing my own sanity now.

With a dejected heart, I go home to rest. Because

as much as I hate it, I'm a mortal, and my body demands certain things.

———

Day bleeds into night and then back again, but I'm relentless, fueled by the fire she's ignited within me. Each morning, I wake with her name on my lips, and each night, I prowl the streets, hitting all the haunts, all our spots, driven by the unshakeable urge to find her.

"Come on, Selene," I growl to myself as I revisit the alley where we first met, where the shadows cling to the walls like dark secrets. "You can't hide from me forever."

The routine is maddening, yet it's become my new normal. I roam, I search, I wait. My mind replays every encounter, every electric touch, every fleeting glance. It's enough to drive a man mad, but I'm already past the point of no return.

I'm hooked, ensnared by a vampiress who's more addictive than any drug, and I'll be damned if I give up now. Selene has got me on a string, and I'll dance to her tune until she decides to show yourself again.

I return to the rose vendor every day. I'm his most loyal customer now.

Because I leave a rose on Selene's doorstep every night.

I watch as they gather, the new ones fresh, the old ones wilted.

I won't give up.

NINE

Selene

I perch atop the crumbling facade of an old bookstore, my gaze trailing Marcus as he weaves his way through the maze of shadows below. The city's pulse thrums beneath my skin, a symphony of heartbeats and whispers, but it's his rhythm that ensnares me—a relentless drumming that echoes his insatiable desire to find me.

"Come on, Selene, where are you?" he murmurs, more to himself than anyone else, and I can't help the way his desperation pulls at my heart. My icy blue eyes track him, this mortal with piercing green eyes that seem to cut through the night, his confident stride a stark contrast to the skulking figures around him.

He's clueless, really. Unaware of how his lifeblood sings to the creatures lurking in these alleys. It's like watching a lamb trot into a lion's den, and it's all sorts of adorable and infuriating.

Marcus, you stubborn, beautiful idiot.

I'm about to swoop down, maybe give him a scare—try to ward him away becuase he's in *the* most dangerous part of the city—but then it happens.

He turns the corner, and there he is—a vampire, one of those low-level goons, all fangs and no finesse. His eyes glow with hunger, the kind that's felt the pang of starvation for far too long. He snarls, a guttural sound that ripples through the damp air, and lunges at Marcus with claws ready to tear into something warm, something alive.

"Shit," I mutter under my breath.

Marcus stands there, frozen for a split second, which is about as long as it takes for any normal person to realize they're in deep trouble. But then, there's nothing normal about Marcus, is there? He dodges, a move that's impressively quick for someone who doesn't spend their nights hunting—or being hunted.

The vampire hisses, and I make my move.

In the blink of an eye, I'm there—between Marcus and a death blow. No grand entrance, just shadows that cling to me like a second skin until I step out. The fellow vampire, all fang and fury, doesn't even see me coming.

But then, they never do. I haven't survived as long as I have for nothing.

"Back off," I growl, my voice low and dangerous, a taunt that promises pain. My hand moves in a blur, nails like daggers slicing through the night air. There's a spray of something dark and foul, and he stumbles back, surprise etched on its grotesque face.

"Selene?" Marcus gasps, but I don't have time for sweet reunions.

"Stay behind me," I command, not as a request but as an order born from centuries of survival. He nods, his green eyes wide with the realization that yes, this is real, and hell yes, it's dangerous.

The vampire recovers, snarling, but it's already over. I lunge, a dance of death honed to perfection over endless nights. There's a snap, a curse, a body hitting the ground with a finality that echoes in the empty alley.

"Damn, Selene... you're..." Marcus trails off, his gaze locked on mine, and I can feel the weight of his words hanging between us, unspoken but understood.

Our eyes lock, and there's this electric charge, this pull I can't deny.

"Here." He breathes out, relief mixing with something else, something hotter, more primal.

"Are you hurt?" I ask, scanning him for injuries, because God, if something happened to him because of me...

"No. Thanks to you," he replies, his voice rough around the edges, like he's trying to stay calm but his body's shouting otherwise. "You were gone, and I—I had to find you."

"Of course you did," I say, softening despite myself. "But you're not invincible, Marcus."

"Neither are you," he counters, and the concern in his eyes tugs at something deep inside me. Something I thought was long dead.

"Let's not test that theory tonight, okay?" I say, and the corner of his mouth lifts in that half-smile that does funny things to my heart.

"Okay," he agrees, and for a moment, we just stand there, in the aftermath, the world narrowing down to just the two of us. And it's terrifying. Because I know I can't walk away from him.

Not again.

Not *ever*.

So, I reach for Marcus's hand, my fingers sliding between his with the ease of long-forgotten intimacy. Without a word, I tug him away from the scene of the fight, each step away from danger and deeper into the city's heart a silent promise of safety. The streets twist and turn, a maze only I navigate with confidence, designed to confuse any who might follow.

We move quickly, our footsteps a hushed rhythm against the cobblestones. Finally, we reach the door to my lair nestled between the shadows.

We step over the roses Marcus has left me every day.

Yes, I watched him leave them daily, my heart breaking the entire time.

With a gentle push, the door gives way, and I guide him into the warm embrace of my lair.

Tapestries older than his lineage drape over stone, their threads telling stories of a time when myth and reality were one. The candles flicker as I lead him deeper into the room, their flames casting dancing silhouettes that play upon the walls. I release his hand, suddenly aware of how mundane my hidden haven must seem. But then he looks at me, and the way his green eyes glimmer in the candlelight sends a shiver down my spine.

The candlelight flickers, casting shadows that dance over Marcus's face, enhancing the green in his eyes—those windows to a soul I'm dangerously close to claiming as my own.

Marcus's gaze never leaves mine. There's a question in his eyes, a silent plea.

"Selene," he starts, his voice barely above a breath, "I—"

"Shh." I place a finger against his lips, stilling his words. There's no need for them now. Everything we need to say is written in the charged air crackling between us.

I'm tired of fighting this.

Our eyes lock, and it's like we're the only two people in the world—or at least, the only two that matter. His pulse quickens beneath my touch, a thrumming beat that syncs with my own undead heart. It's crazy, this connection, this electric pull that tugs at the very core of me.

"Marcus," I breathe out, my name for him a caress all its own.

The space between us evaporates as I lean in, the heat from his body mingling with mine. I can feel his anticipation, a mirror of my own, and it's intoxicating. My lips find his with an urgency that's raw, primal—a hunger that's been simmering just below the surface.

And oh, when our lips meet, it's like the first drop of rain after a century-long drought. It's searing, hot enough to burn, yet I've never felt more alive. My hands roam over his shoulders, pulling him closer, needing him like I need the night sky.

Marcus responds with a fervor that sends a thrill through me. His arms wrap around me, strong and sure, as if he's meant to hold me for all eternity.

And maybe he is.

Our bodies entwine, a perfect fit, and I want to lose myself in the sheer intensity of us.

It's a kiss that speaks of dark nights and whispered promises, of a passion too fierce to be tamed.

And in this moment, in the embrace of shadows and candlelight, I know I'd risk eternity itself for the blaze that Marcus ignites within me.

Garments slip away, discarded carelessly onto the cool stone floor. Our fervor strips us bare, urgency eclipsing all else as we move together—a dance as ancient as time itself. It's skin on skin, his warmth radiating against my eternal chill. The contrast is exquisite, a sensation that ripples through me in waves of pleasure.

"Selene," Marcus breathes out between kisses that trail fire along my collarbone. His touch is electric, sending sparks of need sizzling through my veins.

"Marcus," I gasp back, my voice a mere whisper lost amidst the sound of our rapid breathing. Our movements are frenzied yet synchronized, an exploration that knows no boundaries.

I climb on top of him and slide him inside my wet heat.

We moan in unison, and then I ride him with an abandon I've never know in all my lifetimes.

Marcus's cock hits that perfect spot inside me, and I pulsate around him.

He gasps as his mortal seed floods my dead womb.

For centuries, I've craved this connection, and now it consumes me, devouring every thought that isn't him, isn't us.

He moves with a passion that matches my own, each caress stoking the flames higher. I'm lost in the rhythm of his heartbeat drumming against my chest, a reminder of the life force that pulses within him. His hands roam over my body, worshiping every curve as if committing them to memory.

We're tangled together, the outside world nonexistent. Here, in the cocoon of my lair, only this moment matters. Only the way he looks at me, like I'm both the storm and the shelter all at once.

"God, Selene," Marcus groans, his voice laced with desire and something deeper, something that tugs at the edges of my soul. "I want to be with you, like this, forever."

His words pierce through the haze of pleasure, and for a moment, I falter. The weight of his plea anchors me back to reality, grounding me with its gravity.

"Make me yours, completely," he whispers, his green eyes intense, searching. "Turn me."

The earnestness in his voice sends a jolt through me, sharper than any fang's bite. This is what he wants—to be bound to me for eternity. The idea is tempting, a fantasy I've entertained in moments of weakness. But the implication of his request slices through the passion-fueled fog in my mind.

"Marcus..." My heart thunders against my ribs, a war drum signaling an internal battle.

I shake my head and brace my hands on his chest as I look down at him, my resolve set.

"No."

TEN

Marcus

I can't believe she just said no. No? After everything, after the way our bodies sang together under the sliver of the crescent moon? My heart's pounding a wild rhythm, a symphony of desperation.

Screw it. I won't take no for an answer.

"Selene," I plead one last time, my voice barely a whisper lost in the vastness of her gothic lair.

But she's all ice queen, those baby blues frosted over.

So, I lunge for the knife on the mantelpiece, my

fingers wrapping around the cool handle. Damn, it trembles like a leaf in a storm, but I'm set on this crazy gamble.

"Marcus, what are you—" She cuts herself off as her gaze drops to the blade in my grip.

"Can't live without you, Selene. Literally." I try to crack a smile, but who am I kidding? This is so not the time for jokes.

Her eyes—they do something funny then, widening until they're almost comical. But nothing's funny about the horror that paints her perfect features, the kind of look that says 'oh shit' in every language.

"Marcus, don't!" The words tear from her throat, raw and edged with a fear that doesn't fit her immortal badassery.

"Too late for cold feet, babe." My heart's a jack-hammer, but there's no turning back now. It's do or die—or, well, undead I guess.

Everything slows down, the moment stretching out like some sick joke.

"Sorry, love," I grunt through gritted teeth, and then it's just me and the steel in my hand. The knife feels like it weighs a ton, but my grip is ironclad, fueled by a twisted sense of necessity. With a heave of breath that tastes like finality, I jam the knife into my chest, cold biting hot.

"Ah!" My gasp bounces off stone walls, echoes like a death knell. The pain—it's a beast, clawing its way through my insides, ripping through muscle and memory. Darkness edges my vision, hungry and impatient.

"Marcus!" Selene's scream slams into me, almost as hard as the blade. It's raw, ripped open, and goddamn if it doesn't make me feel victorious and pathetic all at once.

Her hands are on me now—cool, trembling, desperate. Her touch sends shocks of something that's not entirely pain skittering across my skin. But her face, Jesus, it's a portrait of horror painted with a master's hand, those icy blues melting for the first time in front of me.

"Stay with me," she pleads, voice shattered, and I want to laugh because isn't this what I wanted? To shake her, to stir something, anything, in that eternal heart of hers?

"Didn't...plan on...going anywhere..." I manage, my voice a threadbare whisper, every word a sprinter in a marathon I'm losing fast.

"Marcus, you idiot, you..." The rest of her words

get drowned out by the pulse throbbing in my ears—the grand finale before the curtain falls.

But I catch her eyes again, and damn, there's an ocean there, a storm about to break. And I think, I hope, I might just have sparked something—a wildfire in the ice.

Blood pulses under my skin, a drumbeat slowing to the final, mournful thuds as I lock eyes with Selene. The room's shadows cling to her like lovers, but there's no hiding the storm brewing in those glacial blues of hers.

"Selene," I rasp out, each word laced with a cocktail of pain and iron-willed determination. "You've got a choice to make."

Her hands flutter over the wound, slick with my blood, her touch more electric than any mortal's ever could be. She's always been the one with power, the one who decides who gets the gift of darkness eternal. But now...now the tables have turned.

"Let me die, or..." I trail off, coughing up a crimson laugh, "...make me like you. Eternal. Immortal."

The scorn she's worn like armor cracks, just for a split second, revealing the tangle of emotions beneath. Love, fear, anger—they dance in her eyes, a silent ballet that only I'm privy to.

"Damn you, Marcus," she whispers, the words torn from somewhere deep and secret. Her fangs catch the dim light as she leans forward, the lethal points of her dilemma poised above my neck.

I'm not sure if it's the blood loss or the situation's sheer insanity, but I can't help the crooked grin that stretches across my face.

Then her teeth sink into my flesh, sharp and sudden. It's agony and ecstasy, pain blooming into something else entirely—a desperate prayer answered in a language of flesh and fang. Selene's actions ripple through me—devotion written in her every move, desperation etched between each drop of blood we share.

"Fuck," I gasp as the last vestiges of humanity cling to me. "That's...some kiss."

The world doesn't fade. It sharpens, each sensation magnified until it's all I can do not to scream. My blood is hers, and in this moment, so is my soul.

The pain rips through me, a thousand biting ice shards eclipsed only by the heat of Selene's blood as it floods my veins. It's like I'm being torn apart and stitched back together all at once—every cell screaming in rebellion before sighing into surrender. My body convulses, a marionette jerked on strings of fire and frost.

"Selene," I gasp, my voice a raspy echo of the man I used to be moments ago. The room spins, but I'm anchored by her gaze—those icy blue eyes that have seen centuries come and go. Now they're here, watching my every shudder, my every gut-wrenching twist of transformation.

"Stay with me, Marcus." Her voice is a lifeline thrown across the abyss that yawns within me, threatening to swallow me whole.

I claw at the ground, at my own skin, anything to stay present, to not get lost in the maelstrom of rebirth. I've never known agony like this—it's a symphony played on raw nerves, a crescendo of pain that promises an eternity of power. But there's something else too—a rush, a thrill that courses through the torment. It's life...no, more than life. It's life amplified, life eternal.

"Fuck, Selene, what is this?" I manage between convulsions. It's a hurricane. It's a wildfire. It's the birth of a new goddamn universe inside my ribcage.

"Your new beginning," she replies, her voice a silken thread amidst the chaos.

Every heave of my chest feels like the last, until, gradually, the tempest subsides. The pain crystallizes into something sharp and exquisite—a pinpoint of sensation that flares, then winks out, leaving behind a clarity that pierces the murky shadows of my former mortality.

Then, suddenly, stillness.

I lie there, panting, my heart a silent vault within my chest. I don't need it anymore—this dead weight that once throbbed with human frailty. I am beyond, above...other. New senses unfurl within me, and the world blooms into a spectrum of scents and sounds I never knew existed.

"Marcus," Selene breathes, and her voice is the most beautiful thing I've ever heard. "Look at me."

Our eyes meet, and the connection is electric, a circuit completed that fuses our souls with a spark. Relief washes over her face, chased quickly by love— the kind that's been tempered in the forge of sacrifice. We understand each other now, in ways words could never encompass.

The room crackles, charged with a raw, pulsing energy that thrums through my veins like a drumbeat. I'm acutely aware of every inch of Selene's body against mine, the cool silk of her skin a stark contrast to the heat of our passion. She's furious, eyes blazing with an icy fire that should scare me—but it doesn't. Because now, I'm her match in every delicious way.

"Marcus," she hisses, her voice a blend of anger and want. "You reckless fool."

"Reckless?" I drawl, grinning with all the cockiness of the undead. "I prefer 'daring'."

Selene growls, but there's a tremor of desire in it, a vibration that resonates within me. We clash and meld together in a passionate dance, one that's been centuries in the making for her—and a wild dream come true for me. Our entwined forms are a tangle of limbs and whispers, of sharp teeth and even sharper cravings.

"God, you're infuriating," she breathes out as we move together, fluid and unrestrained. There's an edge to her voice, but it's dulled by the lust that laces each syllable.

"Infuriatingly irresistible," I correct, and I feel her chuckle against my neck, a sensation that sends shivers down my spine.

Our bodies find a rhythm born of ancient instincts and eternal hunger. Each touch is a spark that ignites a deeper yearning, each kiss a promise of endless nights spent exploring the abyss of our desires. Her nails rake along my back, not enough to break the skin, but plenty to mark her territory.

"Yours," I whisper, a pledge wrapped in a single word.

"Mine," she echoes, sealing it with a bite that is both a punishment and a reward. I bite her back.

The taste of her on my tongue is divine—a flavor I want to savor forever.

We lose ourselves in the montage of movement, a symphony of moans and sighs that fills the air. My world narrows down to this moment, to the weight of Selene in my arms, to the intoxicating mix of pleasure and power coursing through us. Every glide and thrust pushes us further into the depths of our newfound immortality, and I revel in the strength that surges within me.

"More," she demands, and I oblige, because how could I not? This is what I wanted—what I chose—the ultimate connection, bound by blood and forged in the fires of damnation. And damn, if it isn't the most exhilarating ride of my afterlife.

"Always more," I vow, and the promise hangs between us, heavy with the certainty that we'll spend eternity chasing the high of this very moment.

The world shatters into a million shards of ecstasy as Selene and I hit the peak together. It's like every cell in my body is firing off fireworks, a riotous celebration of unbridled pleasure that seizes me and shakes me to the core. Our cries mingle, raw and untamed, a primal duet that reverberates against the ancient walls of her chamber.

"Selene!" I gasp, my voice hoarse with the intensity of release, feeling her name carve itself into my soul.

"Marcus," she breathes out, her icy blue eyes ablaze with passion, locked onto mine. Her fangs graze my skin, a delicious sting that sends another shockwave through me.

It's overwhelming, this connection—more than physical, it's spiritual, an entwining of essences that stitches us together across the fabric of eternity. We're not just bodies tangled in the throes of lust anymore. We're two beings fused at the deepest level, our bond immortal.

We collapse, a tangle of limbs and heaving chests, our slick skin glistening under the moon's voyeuristic glow. She's draped over me, her hair cascading around us like a silvery veil. Despite the feverish activity, there's a peace that settles in the space between our panting breaths.

"Damn, Selene," I chuckle, the sound bubbling up from somewhere deep inside, "Who knew eternal damnation could feel this good?"

"Only the damned," she retorts, her lips curving into a sly smile that promises more sin in our future.

We lie there, entwined, savoring the afterglow that only immortals can truly appreciate. Her heartbeat, once silent like the grave, now thrums against me in a steady rhythm—a reminder of the life, or rather the un-life, that courses within us both.

I pull Selene closer, our sweat-drenched bodies melding into one another as if we're trying to burrow into each other's souls. The air around us crackles with the raw energy of our union, and I can't help but think, eternity is going to be amazing.

We make love over and over again, and my body never tires.

It's fucking amazing.

"Ready for round...what is it now? Five? Six?" Selene teases, her voice a sultry melody that sends shivers down my spine, despite the fact that technically, I shouldn't be feeling much cold these days.

"Lost count," I admit with a smirk. "But who's counting anyway? We have all the time in the world, love."

Her laughter rings out, clear and bright, filling the room with the sound of our reckless abandon. It's music to my ears, the kind of tune I could listen to on repeat for centuries to come—and I plan to do exactly that.

Epilogue

Selene

The air thrums with an electric charge as I push open the door to our lair—a sanctuary cloaked in shadows and secrets. Tonight, the darkness feels alive, pulsating with the memory of a momentous collision of souls one year ago.

A single red rose lies on the mahogany table, its velvety petals enigmatic against the polished wood. Beside it, a slip of paper beckons, scrawled ink weaving a poem only Marcus would pen:

*Roses are red
Blood is too
No depth of words could convey
How much I love you.*

The corners of my lips lift into a smile—it's been centuries since anyone has chiseled through the ice of my vampiric heart.

I pivot on my heel, feeling the silken glide of my dress against my thighs, and there he is—Marcus, my mate, my husband, that smirk decorating his lips like he's privy to the world's most sinfully delicious secret. His piercing green eyes are locked on mine, a silent challenge issued in their depths.

"Happy anniversary, Selene." His voice, a dark caress, fills the space between us.

"Marcus," I breathe, allowing the warmth radiating from his soul to wash over me.

He covers the distance in a heartbeat, those immortal limbs of his defying any notion of human fragility. When his arms encircle me, they are bands of iron dressed in velvet, pulling me into a world where I am not just a creature of the night but *his* creature, his partner in this eternal dance.

"Forever and a day," he vows against my lips, and

I melt into the kiss, our mouths speaking the language of undying love and carnal need.

Marcus' hands roam with a possessiveness that sets every nerve ending ablaze, his touch both a balm and a blaze. He guides me backward until my knees hit the edge of the bed—the very place where two worlds collided and became one.

"Let me show you eternity," he murmurs as he lowers me onto the silk sheets.

His mouth descends, trailing fiery kisses down my body, unwrapping me like the greatest gift he's ever received. The cool night air of our lair contrasts with the heat of his breath as he parts my thighs with a reverence reserved for the sacred.

And then, oh god, then—his tongue finds me, and the universe narrows down to the point of his desire. My back arches off the bed, a silent plea for more, always more. There's no thought, only sensation. No past or future, only now, as Marcus worships at the altar of my body with a fervor that could outshine the sun.

"Marcus..." His name is a litany on my lips, a prayer to the night, as pleasure coils tight within me. I'm falling, tumbling into a chasm of ecstasy, where time loses meaning, and love is an unspoken vow renewed with each stroke of his tongue.

Tonight, we celebrate not just an anniversary but the affirmation of an immortal love—a love that transcends lifetimes, a love that redefines what it means to exist. And here, in our lair, we surrender to it wholly, fiercely, eternally.

When I finally come down from my blinding orgasm, I open my eyes to see Marcus grinning down at me smugly.

I'll show him...

I shove Marcus back with a force that resonates through the ancient walls of our lair, his green eyes flashing with that mix of surprise and insatiable hunger I adore. He lands with a predatory grace, a smirk playing on his lips, as he stretches out on the bed like a feast awaiting my indulgence.

"Your turn," I purr, crawling over him with the elegance of night itself. My fingers trail down his sculpted chest, tracing the lines of his muscles before I find the waistband of his pants. With a flick of my wrist, they're gone, and I'm greeted by the sight of his arousal—proud and inviting.

"God, Selene, don't tease." His voice is a growl, laced with desire and impatience.

"Tease?" I echo, feigning innocence as I lean in, my cool breath brushing against him. "I haven't even started."

My mouth closes around him, slow and deliberate, taking him in inch by inch. The taste of him is intoxicating—a flavor that speaks to centuries of longing, a reminder of the life that pulses beneath his skin. He's hard and hot, a stark contrast to my eternal chill, and I savor the difference.

"Fuck, yes..." Marcus hisses as I swirl my tongue, drawing a line up the underside of his cock. I increase the rhythm, sucking harder, deeper, driven by the sounds he makes—the sharp intakes of breath, the whispered curses. They're music to my vampiric senses, a symphony of pleasure that I conduct with lips and tongue.

His hands find their way into my hair, guiding me, urging me on. I take him fully, swallowing around him, feeling him twitch and pulse in my throat. And then there's that sweet moment where control slips away from him, his essence flooding my mouth in a rush that I welcome, drinking him down like the rarest vintage.

"Selene, I need—"

But he doesn't have to finish the sentence, because I already know. Lust courses through me— a fierce, unyielding tide—as I rise to meet him. Our bodies collide with the inevitability of stars crashing together, my hot heat sliding onto his hardness, creating new constellations with each thrust.

"Mine," he grunts, pounding into me with a fervency that speaks of eternal vows and undying passion.

"Yours," I gasp, nails raking down his back, marking him as surely as he marks my soul.

We move together, a dance as old as time, yet fresh with the thrill of the now. Each stroke stokes the fire within us, each moan a testament to a love that cannot be tamed or contained. I feel the crescendo building, that electric tension that promises release—and when it hits, it's cataclysmic.

"Marcus!"

"Selene!"

Our names become a shared cry as we come together, our climax shattering the silence of the lair, echoing through the shadows. In this moment, we are one—undying and unstoppable, a force of nature that not even time can erode.

As we collapse into each other's arms, spent and sated, I can't help but think that eternity never felt so damn good.

. . .

Want more Kenzie Skye? Go to www.authorkenzieskye.com.